P9-CEI-089

Dear Parents and Teachers,

In an easy-reader format, **My Readers** introduce classic stories to children who are learning to read. Although favorite characters and time-tested tales are the basis for **My Readers**, the books tell completely new stories and are freshly and beautifully illustrated.

My Readers are available in three levels:

1 **Level One** is for the emergent reader and features repetitive language and word clues in the illustrations.

2 **Level Two** is for more advanced readers who still need support saying and understanding some words. Stories are longer with word clues in the illustrations.

3 **Level Three** is for independent, fluent readers who enjoy working out occasional unfamiliar words. The stories are longer and divided into chapters.

Encourage children to select books based on interests, not reading levels. Read aloud with children, showing them how to use the illustrations for clues. With adult guidance and rereading, children will eventually read the desired book on their own.

Here are some ways you might want to use this book with children:

- Talk about the title and the cover illustrations. Encourage the child to use these to predict what the story is about.
- Discuss the interior illustrations and try to piece together a story based on the pictures. Does the child want to change or adjust his first prediction?
- After children reread a story, suggest they retell or act out a favorite part.

My Readers will not only help children become readers, they will serve as an introduction to some of the finest classic children's books available today.

—LAURA ROBB
Educator and Reading Consultant

An Imprint of Macmillan Children's Publishing Group

 Distributed in Canada by H.B. Fenn and Company Ltd.
Printed in January 2011 in China by Toppan Leefung Printing Ltd.,
Dongguan City, Guangdong Province.
For information, address Square Fish, 175 Fifth Avenue, New York, NY 10010.

Library of Congress Cataloging-in-Publication Data Available

ISBN: 978-0-312-62484-2 (hardcover)
1 3 5 7 9 10 8 6 4 2

ISBN: 978-0-312-62485-9 (paperback)
1 3 5 7 9 10 8 6 4 2

Book design by Patrick Collins/Véronique Lefèvre Sweet

Square Fish logo designed by Filomena Tuosto

First Edition: 2011

www.squarefishbooks.com
www.mackids.com

This is a Level 1 book

LEXILE 290L

CARL and the BABY DUCK

story and pictures by

Alexandra Day

SQUARE FISH

Macmillan Children's Publishing Group

New York

One of Carl's friends
needs help.
Who can it be?

It's Mama Duck.

A baby duck is missing.

Mama Duck goes one way
to look for Baby Duck.

Carl goes another way.

Is Baby Duck in the flowers?

No, only a worm is there.

Is Baby Duck in the bush?

No, only a bird is there.

Is Baby Duck
behind the bench?

No, only a cat is there.

Is Baby Duck
at the playground?

It doesn't look like
Baby Duck is here.

Maybe Baby Duck
is in the tunnel.

No, only two boys are there.

Here comes Carl's friend Lucy.

“Lucy, have you seen
Baby Duck?”

No, Lucy has not seen
Baby Duck.

Where could Baby Duck be?

Carl thinks of one more place to look.

Carl jumps into the fountain
to look for Baby Duck.

There's Baby Duck!

“Let’s go home, Baby Duck,”
says Carl.

Mother Duck is so happy to see them.

What a good dog, Carl.